This book belongs to

....

PUFFIN BOOKS

UK | USA | Canada | Ireland | Australia
India | New Zealand | South Africa

Puffin Books is part of the Penguin Random House group of companies whose addresses can be found at global.
penguinrandomhouse.com.

puffinbooks.com

Penguin
Random House
UK

First published 2015
001

Text and illustrations copyright © Activision Publishing, Inc., 2015
Written by Cavan Scott
Illustrations by Dani Geremia (Beehive Agency)

Printed in China

A CIP catalogue record for this book is available from the British Library

ISBN: 978–0–141–35851–2

Contents

Trinket Trail
These ten trinkets have been hidden somewhere in your annual. Jot down the page numbers when you find them!

10 THINGS
YOU NEED TO KNOW ABOUT
SKYLANDS!

Hello, Portal Master!
I am Onk Beakman, voted Skylands'
top penguin author by 'Penguins Today'
magazine for four years running.
Here's a handy guide to the top ten
things you need to know about our
magical realm.

Onk

1 Skylands is slap-bang in the middle of the universe. You can't miss it. Look for magic and adventure, and there it is!

2 It is made up of millions and gazillions of floating islands. Some are beautiful and some are beastly, but all are bursting with excitement. Oh, and sheep. Lots and lots of sheep.

3 From Skylands, you can hop anywhere in the cosmos – which is why an evil Portal Master by the name of Kaos is determined to conquer Skylands. He's also determined to find a cure for his baldness, but just imagine how silly he'd look with hair! Why not give him your own crazy hairstyle in the picture to the right?

4 Kaos isn't the only villain in Skylands. Many evildoers used to be locked up in Cloudcracker Prison – until Kaos shattered its Traptanium walls using the Fork of Infinite Resonance, and every fiend escaped, that is! Disaster!

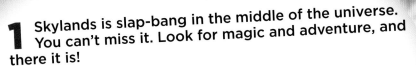

5 Don't worry! Skylands is protected by the Skylanders, the most heroic heroes in the history of heroism.

6 Each Skylander is linked to an Elemental force that gives them amazing powers. The Elements are Air, Earth, Water, Fire, Tech, Magic, Life, Undead, Light and Dark.

7 The Skylanders are also helped by loyal friends such as Flynn the pilot. The other day, Flynn told me how much he loved my books. Then I found out he was only using them to stop his mirror from wobbling. He can spend hours looking at his reflection, that one.

8 Flynn is still hoping an Enchilada Element will be found. I fear he is to be disappointed.

9 Skylanders learn how to use their powers at the newly opened Skylanders Academy, under the guidance of legendary Skylander trainer, Buzz. It's odd – Buzz reminds me of someone, but I can't think who!

10 Skylanders also need Portal Masters like you! Only you can help keep the forces of the Darkness at bay! The future of Skylands is in your hands, so I hope you've washed them. I can't stand dirty hands . . .

ATTACK

Which Skylander are you most like?
Do you plough right in using brute force,
prefer to blow things up or surprise
everyone with a sneaky stealth attack?
Answer the questions to find out!

Try to kick it open!

When they explode! They do explode, don't they?

Sometimes!

Blast it into little tiny pieces!

Super strength!

Is blowing stuff up a super power? If so, that!

START

Don't know. I can't hear them because I'm so noisy!

Invisibility!

Of course! The louder the better!

Yes!

Nope! I prefer the quiet!

No! Not my style!

FORCE!

Rugby!

Ripping open the wrapping paper!

With a hammer!

Darts (using homing missiles, natch!)

Picking him up and chucking him all the way to the Outlands!

YOU USE BRUTE FORCE LIKE WALLOP! *CRASH!*

With a stick of dynamite!

Hiding a grenade in his cocoa!

YOU BLOW THINGS SKY HIGH LIKE COUNTDOWN! *BOOM!*

I don't like crisps! They make too much noise!

Nope! I can't stay still long enough!

Sneaking up behind him and shouting "BOO!"

Not really!

The best!

YOU LAUNCH STEALTH ATTACKS LIKE STEALTH ELF! *SHHHHHH!*

9

MAD HATTERS

by Onk Beakman

PART ONE: GET AHEAD, GET A HAT!

"**W**oah! What's the hurry?" Torch the Fire Skylander picked herself up from where Fling Kong had knocked her flying. The excitable monkey hopped up and down as he gabbled his apologies.

"Sorry, sorry, sorry!" he said. "It's just so exciting!"

"What is?" Torch asked, still none the wiser. She had been practising with her Firespout Flamethrower in the grounds of Skylanders Academy when Fling had barged into her. And, come to think of it, he wasn't the only one hurrying about. Everywhere Torch looked, Skylanders were busily charging around. What was going on?

"Surely you haven't forgotten?" Fling Kong asked. "It's the Academy Hat Competition today!" Fling looked at Torch's head of flaming hair. "You have got a hat, right?"

Steam blew out of Torch's nose as she snorted an unconvincing laugh. "Me? Of course I have!"

"You better grab it then," said Flynn, racing off across the lawn. "Master Eon's going to start judging in a few minutes!"

Torch's heart sank as she watched the Mabu pilot scamper off. She hadn't been completely honest with the manic monkey. She had been so busy training with her Firespout that she'd completely forgotten about the contest. She had nothing to wear.

Suddenly, a thought occurred to her. "Hatterson," she said aloud, already making for the doors of the Main Hall. "He'll be able to sell me a hat! His hat store is full of them!"

But, when Torch got to the Upper Hallway, the hat-maker was closing up his shop.

"Sorry," he sniffed. "I'm out of stock. Trigger Happy bought the last hat five minutes ago."

Oh no! Torch thought, watching her fellow Skylanders dart around, all proudly wearing their hats.

"Stop skull-king around, Torch!" barked Funny Bone, as he charged down the stairs from the Games Room wearing a jaunty Viking Helmet. The Undead skele-dog suddenly sniggered. "Hey, that reminds me – what do you call a lazy skeleton?"

Torch shrugged, preparing herself for one of Funny Bone's gags. The mirthful mutt was always cracking awful rib-ticklers, whatever the situation.

"BONE IDLE!" Funny Bone laughed. "Geddit?"

An ever-so-slightly flustered Food Fight came running past from the other direction. "We haven't time for jokes," he said. "I lost my favourite Banana Hat to Dreadbeard in a game of Skystones Smash. I'm off to win it back!"

Then something very odd happened. With a flash of light, a large green hatbox appeared in front of Food Fight.

"Where did that come from?" he asked, as another box popped into existence in front of Funny Bone.

"I've got one too!" Torch said in amazement, peering at yet another hatbox that hadn't been there a second before.

"What are we waiting for?" said Food Fight. "Let's find out what's inside!"

Funny Bone didn't need to be told twice. The skeletal dog was already tearing at his box's shiny ribbon. Torch did the same, ripping the lid off and gasping as a glowing hat rose into the air. It was shaped like a candle, complete with a brightly burning flame.

"Wow!" she said. "That's hot stuff!"

"Not as good as mine," barked Funny Bone, who had already swapped his Viking Helmet for the sparkling Skull Cap that had emerged from his hatbox. "What do you think?" he asked.

"Not bad," said Food Fight, who was trying on a top hat shaped like a ripe, red tomato. "Winning back my Banana Hat has lost its a-peel! This new one is already growing on me!"

Torch popped her Candle Hat on to her head. It fitted perfectly, almost as if it had been made for her.

"Looking good, Torch," said Funny Bone. "Say, that reminds me – what did one candle say to the other candle?"

Food Fight couldn't help but roll his eyes.

"Are you going out tonight?" Funny Bone delivered his punchline with relish.

"Your jokes are enough to get on anyone's wick," said Food Fight, with a good-humoured smirk.

"Ha! Let's go!" yelled Funny Bone, charging towards the doors to the academy grounds. "Nobody is going to be able to beat me now, especially while Food Fight's wearing that thing. It makes him look a real fruit loop!"

"Ha!" Food Fight said, chasing after him. "You'll eat those words when my hat is crowned cream of the crop!"

"I'm just ribbing you," shot back Funny Bone. "Let's make a break for it!"

Torch smiled as her friends teased each other. She knew that her hat was the best – or at least it had been when she'd put it on! Something wet splashed against her cheek, and Torch looked up in horror to see that the heat of her fiery hair had melted her Candle Hat.

"It's ruined," she moaned, pulling the molten mess from her head. As the wax dribbled through her fingers, another idea occurred to her. "Funny Bone's Viking Helmet!" She laughed, running back to the Upper Hallway. "He doesn't want it any more. I'm sure he won't mind if I borrow it!"

***

Funny Bone didn't even notice the ill-fitting Viking helmet when Torch finally joined the others outside. The Undead Skylander was too busy gaping at Fling Kong desperately trying to pull his brand new Frisbee Hat off his head.

"I don't understand," said Fling. "It fitted perfectly when I found it in that hatbox, but now it's far too tight!"

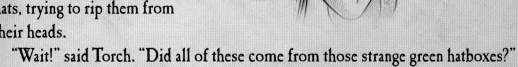

Beside him, Food Fight tugged at his Tomato Top Hat. "Hey, mine won't budge either. It's squashed tight on my head!" he said.

All around, Skylanders were struggling with their hats, trying to rip them from their heads.

"Wait!" said Torch. "Did all of these come from those strange green hatboxes?"

The Skylanders didn't have a chance to answer. With a series of loud pops, each and every hat transformed into a garish Chompy hat!

"Hey," complained Food Fight. "That's not to my taste at . . ."

His voice trailed off as his face fell slack. Torch glanced around at Fling Kong and Funny Bone. Their expressions were the same: completely and utterly blank.

"Hahahahaaaaaa!" cackled a familiar voice. Torch whirled round to see the Chompy Mage standing behind them, waving his Chompy-topped staff.

"My plan worked," the mad magician crowed to his ever-present Chompy glove puppet. "The Skylanders fell for it! They're all wearing my mind-control Chompy Caps!"

The glove puppet uttered a shrill giggle. "Who is your master now?" the puppet said to the blank-faced Skylanders.

Torch couldn't believe her ears when her friends all replied as one:

"We obey the Chompy Maaaage!"

Oh no! The Skylanders are under the Chompy Mage's spell. Turn to page 48 to find out what happens next!

Skylanders BATTLE BINGO

Fill out these Skylands bingo cards next time you're playing a game of Skylanders. Why not challenge a friend? Who can complete their card first?

You see a flying fish!	Kaos says someone is doomed!	You meet a Gillman!
You solve a prism puzzle!	Flynn says "Boom!"	You push a turtle!
You use a Bounce Pad!	You see a Molekin!	You open a gate with two or more keys!

You find a Legendary Treasure!	You meet a Mabu!	You see Persephone!
You see a battle gate!	You open a Lockmaster gate or door!	Kaos insults the Portal Master!
You see a slice of pizza!	You see Hugo!	You fight a troll!

How to play:

1. You and a friend choose a card each.
2. Play any of the Skylanders games.
3. When you spot something mentioned on your card, put a coin on that box.
4. The winner is the first person to cross everything off on their card! Good luck!

You see Glumshanks! 	You grab a coin!	You find a Winged Sapphire!
You fight a cyclops!	Flynn pilots an airship!	You find an Elemental Gate!
You see a hot-air balloon!	You level up!	You have to push something that *isn't* a turtle!

You find a Treasure Chest!	You meet Auric!	You see a sheep!
You have to play a card or stones game!	You find a Story Scroll!	Flynn tries to impress Cali!
Kaos insults a Skylander!	You open a locked gate!	Chompies attack!

Word Portal

Can you unscramble the Skylanders' names and then find them in the wordsearch?

ABT NSPI
OLBKUTCA
DSBALE
TBMNDILRASE
KBSAUHWHC
POCHREP
RABCO DBARAAC
JEDA UV
HCOE
GIMENA
SIFT PUBM
NLFIG NOKG
PIFL CREWK
OFOD HIGTF
YRNFO
NUFYN EBON
GFTERIASH
LIGL NUTRG
SUTOG
ADHE HSRU
GIHH VIFE

ABEKRJWRAE
JTE-CVA
OMAKBO
TGNHIK TGLIH
KIHNGT RAME
TYPRK NIKG
BOL-RTSA
PPO ZIFZ
ORKYC LRLO
RTOHS TCU
OOOBRMSHMO
PNAS TOSH
SOLTPGITH
NDRLBTOEUTH
HCRTO
TARLI ZLBAER
DETRA EHDA
FUTF CUKL
PLWOAL
DLIWRFIE

NEED HELP?
Want to skip straight to the wordsearch without solving the anagrams? Hold the bottom of the page up to a mirror!

BAT SPIN
BLACKOUT
BLADES
BLASTERMIND
BUSHWHACK
CHOPPER
COBRA CADABRA
DEJA VU
ECHO
ENIGMA

FIST BUMP
FLING KONG
FLIP WRECK
FOOD FIGHT
FRYNO
FUNNY BONE
GEARSHIFT
GILL GRUNT
GUSTO
HEAD RUSH

HIGH FIVE
JAWBREAKER
JET-VAC
KABOOM
KNIGHT LIGHT
KNIGHT MARE
KRYPT KING
LOB-STAR
POP FIZZ
ROCKY ROLL

SHORT CUT
SHROOMBOOM
SNAP SHOT
SPOTLIGHT
THUNDERBOLT
TORCH

TRAIL BLAZER
TREAD HEAD
TUFF LUCK
WALLOP
WILDFIRE

16

PLUS:
How many times is 'HAT' hidden in the grid?

```
C Y M C I M N G F E V B V O T B W R O U T K U H Z B T H Y D
I O D O B X W I N K D L U E F L L R E B H W G A D R F S Z V
B W B P O P F I Z Z E A B S I Y I A Q Z H T O T E Y E U Q M
X N F R C N G X Y Q J S P Q H B L X D U A G N A M V C R S T
I J R G A M E V G Y A T J A S W V E W E N L D P I J U D N N
R O M V A C R V U R V E E O R I H K C I S H B F B U G A A W
Y T U O K C A L B N U R G M A S W A K H E Q H L N K M E P V
Z G T H G I F D O O F M O M E D G T C A O G C J I Q K H S T
S H L N B P B I A W P I D C G E P I D K I N M Z P A X E H V
P N Y A N E P O T B K N J N K Y D T A H X H O Z Z I R S O Z
O X B M D I N O J F R D L H R Y A C M I R J K L X F Q T T Y
T C M F F P P O T M D A V K V R R V B I V O Y Q H E H O Y H
L O B S T A R S B A E L T Q Y K X O G U T S F V F T G L T M
I R F O I W P T T Y H A D Z N R H M L S B S X L B E Z J M Y
G E L Y Y P I M Z A N W R I D E Q K U L P U I M S L J Y W F
H P I J E B P S U E B N G T U K L G B W S P E R I F D L I W
T P N C K M Y H R B Y H U Y I A Q G Z M W H O R S V G S M C
C O G P S U A A W Z T G C F G E E H Q R F N O T B U P I G T
L H K Y H K M J T L F S K R A R V G E D W X K R P S N E W U
G C O N L T P K I L K Y I Q T B I C T O R C H O T U Q B Q H
I O N Q H Y O G U K M K L F G W K W W K M A Z P L C Q Y O M
C X G G V Q H U Z O F I O G C A S H R O O M B O O M U H B T
X B I O B T K M O O B A K Z H J Q Q U P C C Q A M T V T J U
S N C G F X C X P R Z O U R V T Y U T N A E P X T U Z O K F
K S R M G I L L G R U N T Z A D B Q A V F P V A I H Z Q W F
X B M R S F N Z Q E U Y E O B H G O T N U O H E W K C H Y L
T L O B R E D N U H T R H A T J Y E K E G F E L E L T A S U
Q O K H X C K B R T U F Y Z Y T J O W P O L L A W I L T B C
F D S E M J F H R L I J N T A M T S M H C R B S P Z T T D K
Y N C B H A T P Y S J G C I U U J W E R X E B V C V L X H D
```

GROSSLANDS

Read on to discover the grossest things in all of Skylands . . . if you dare!

Goo!

Surely the most sickening substance in Skylands, goo is smelly and sticky and distinctly bad for your health. No wonder so many villains use the vile stuff for their dastardly plans. Why does something so powerful need to be so pongy?

The Supreme Sewers of Supreme Stink

Curiously, the Gillmen who work in Skylands' smelliest sewers are terrified of germs – you'd think they'd be used to them. The sewers are also home to the dreaded Slime Eel. This slippery customer leaves a putrid path of pure poison wherever it slithers!

Wrecking Ball

Even Skylanders are gross from time to time. Wrecking Ball may be brave, but he's also full of gas. His burps soon knock the wind out of his enemies (or anyone else unlucky enough to get a whiff, come to think of it). Oh well, better out than in!

Soda

Hold on! Isn't soda supposed to be tasty? Not Bottom-feeding Suction-eel-flavoured Soda. It's ranked 'Most Stomach-churning Soda of All Time' in Professor P. Grungally's classic *1001 Things You Must Never Drink, Even When You're Really Thirsty and There's Nothing Else To Drink*. Snappy title, eh?

DID YOU KNOW?

Bottom-feeding Suction-eel-flavoured Soda was invented by Kaos himself. Figures!

Stink Bomb

Sometimes gross can be good. Life Skylander Stink Bomb has turned his anti-social odour into a musky martial art known as Kung Fume. The Noxious Ninja gives off a bad smell that leaves his foes feeling queasy.

Slobbering Mutticuses

There's one thing worse than being bitten by a Slobbering Mutticus, and that's having a Slobbering Mutticus drool all over you. You'll be stuck in a pool of its disgusting dribble for days.

DID YOU KNOW?

Mohawk Cyclopses use Mutticus slobber to stick their wigs to their bald heads. Perhaps Kaos should try it!

Cyclopses

What a bunch of stinkers! The reason cyclopses smell so bad is because they use lumps of stone instead of soap, and only have a bath once every never.

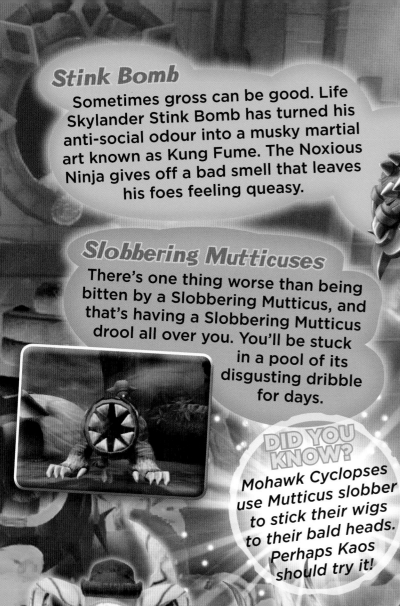

Stealth Skunk

Which of these four shadows perfectly matches Stink Bomb?

A   B   C   D

Cali is on a mission to track down the Gulper, but she needs your help. Can you work out how to crack her clever code?

We'vn eearlf yount ∂hG eulpeH. re'h sidini gt nhv ealleo yt fhS eod∀ aolcanoeG. seF tlynt nf olo yveh rerr eigha twaH! ye't sho enlo ynw ehc oah nelb, pup tleas∂ eon't telh lit mhat!

Write it here:
....
....
....
....
....
....

Use a mirror to discover how to crack Cali's code!

Decode the message by swapping the last letter of one word with the first letter of the next.

Now use the code to write a message to your friends!

Goow dorP kortaM laster!

20

Zoo Lou's Scavenger Hunt

**How good a Skylands scavenger are you?
Play Zoo Lou's dice game to find out!**

How to play:

1 Stick this shape on to a sheet of card.
2 Carefully cut it out, asking an adult to help you.
3 Fold along all the white lines.
4 Stick the tabs down with glue to make a cube. This is your scavenger dice!
5 Take it in turns to roll the dice to see which Skylander you get.
6 You have one minute to find as many things as you can that start with the first letter of the Skylander's name. For example, if you get Spyro, find as many things as you can that begin with the letter 'S'. You can play either in your Skylanders game, or in real life!
7 The player with the most things after a minute wins!

Trigger Happy's Tongue Twisters

Can you say these silly sentences five times in a row without getting your tongue in a twist?

- *Bouncer bounces Bash but Bash bashes back!*
- *Rocky Roll really rates Rubble Rouser's rocks!*
- *Gusto grips ghastly golems!*
- *Star Strike, star bright, star light!*
- *Scorp swipes stealthily while Swarm swoops swiftly!*
- *Kaos can't crack coconuts, but Glumshanks gladly can!*

Can you make up your own tongue twisters?

TREAD HEAD

FLIP WRECK

DROBOT

SPYRO

HEX

BUMBLE BLAST

Join Skylanders Academy!

**Have you got what it takes to become a Skylander?
Take the Academy entrance test and find out!**

1 It's early morning and the Mabu Defence Force sends out an SOS! What do you do?

A Rush to help!

B Roll over and snooze! Another five minutes in bed won't hurt!

C Sing a song!

D Laugh maniacally! You're the reason the MDF sent the SOS in the first place!

2 What do you think about Eon?

A He's the greatest Portal Master of all time! You hope that one day you will be as brave, noble and wise as him!

B Is that the big, floaty ghost-guy? Shudder! He gives you the creeps!

C Does he like singing songs? If so, he's cool!

D Hate him! Hate him! HAAAAATE HIIIMMM!

3 A crystal has been discovered that transforms harmless plants into hideous monsters. What do you do?

A Smash the crystal into tiny little pieces! Now no one will be able to use it for evil!

B Cover the crystal up with a big blanket and hope no one notices!

C Sing a song!

D Transform the academy's flowerbeds into horrendous hungry mouths on stalks! Bwahahahaaaaa!

4 What do you want most of all in life?

A To protect those who cannot protect themselves!

B To be left alone!

C To sing songs!

D UNIVERSAL DOMINATION! (Plus, as many sodas as you can drink.)

5 Molekin miners are trapped deep underground. What do you do next?

A Start digging them out. There's no time to lose!

B Get distracted when you spot a Winged Sapphire nearby. Oooh, shiny!

C Sing a song!

D Use the opportunity to steal all of the miners' things. Well, they can't stop you from down there, can they?

6. A Fire Viper is burning the Tower of Time to its very foundations! What do you do?

A Climb to the top of the tower and try to extinguish the Fire Viper before it can do any more damage.

B Use the heat from the blaze to roast some marshmallows – from a safe distance, obviously.

C Sing a song!

D Adopt the Fire Viper as your new pet.

7. Kaos has discovered an ancient Arkeyan Engine of Extreme Doom! What do you do?

A Stop the evildoer, come what may. Skylands must be protected!

B Have a little panic and hide beneath the table!

C Sing a song!

D Steal the Arkeyan Engine of Extreme Doom from Kaos and then use it yourself! This much evil was wasted on the little squirt, anyway.

8. Cali has been captured – again! What's your first thought?

A I must search every island until I find her!

B Serves her right.

C Can I sing a song about this?

D Curses! You were planning to kidnap her today! You decide to kidnap Tessa instead.

9. Are you completely and utterly evil?

A No!

B No!

C No!

D Yes!

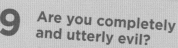

How did you do?

Mostly As: *Boomsticks!* You're a natural Skylander! Welcome to the academy!

Mostly Bs: *Sorry!* Skylandering maybe isn't for you. Perhaps try again when you're a bit more heroic.

Mostly Cs: I think you'd be happier with the Skaletones! You'll find them in the Great Hall.

Mostly Ds: You're obviously an evil maniac in disguise! Try the Doom Raiders instead. Oh, and look out for the Skylanders. They're watching you!

FOOD FRENZY!

The Skylanders are caught in the middle of a fierce battle! Work out which heroes get a health-boosting snack – and who gets the bomb!

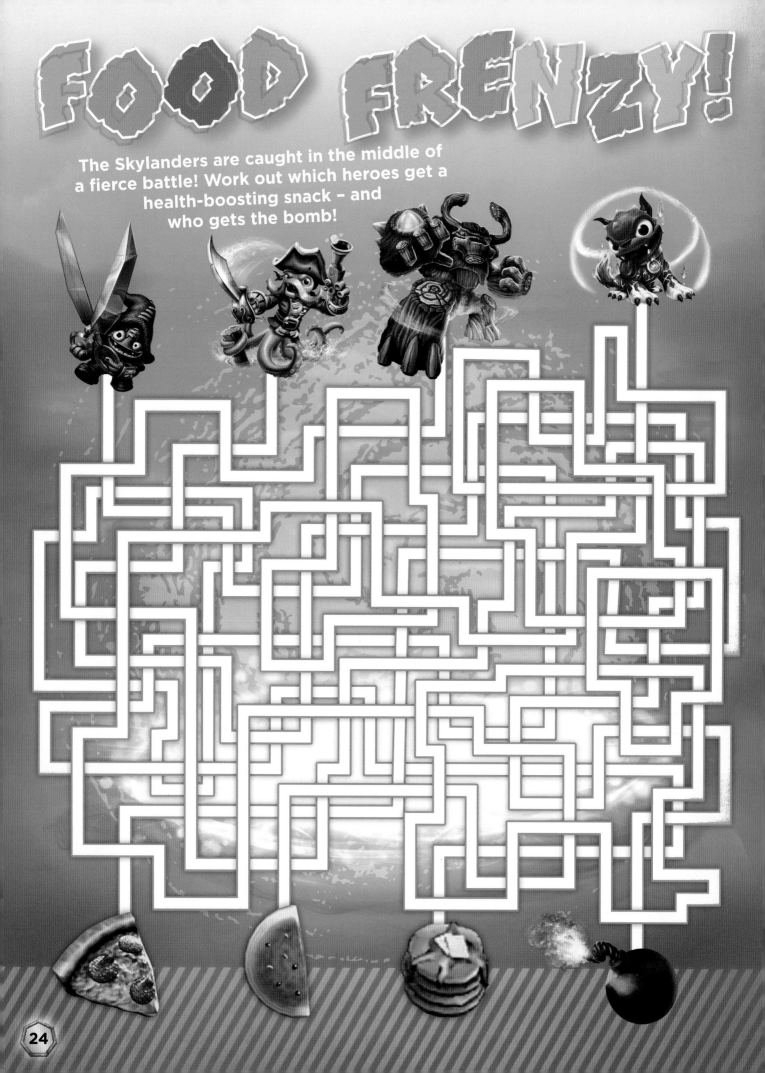

BLASTERMIND'S MEMORY TRAP

How good is your memory? Study this page for one minute, then turn the page and write down as many objects and characters as you can remember! No peeking!

TIME'S UP!
Turn the page and start remembering!

MEMORY DUMP!

OK, grab your pen, pencil or phoenix-chicken-feather quill, and write down as many things as you can remember!

1 ....
2 ....
3 ....
4 ....
5 ....
6 ....
7 ....
8 ....
9 ....
10 ....
11 ....
12 ....
13 ....
14 ....
15 ....
16 ....
17 ....
18 ....
19 ....
20 ....

MINDSTORM

Here are some extra questions to see just how observant you are!

1 What colour were Blastermind's eyes on the previous page?

2 How many crystals could you see on his hat?

3 Was the title of the page blue?

4 How many pairs of wings were there on the page?

Five Minutes with FLYNN

Skylands' greatest pilot talks about himself – what a surprise!

MASTER EON or LORD KAOS?

Are you kidding? That Kaos guy really grinds my gears! Plus, he owes my buddy Terrafin five dollars. I can't stand people who don't pay their debts! What? I owe you a fiver? Er, let me get back to you on that . . .

LAND or SKY?

Hey, Captain Flynn is never happier than when he's up in the great blue yonder. Unless he's up in the great blue yonder with a huge plate of enchiladas, that is! Mmmmmm. Is it lunchtime yet?

TAKING OFF or LANDING?

I'm awesome at both, so it doesn't matter. I'm also surprisingly good at crashing! Bet you didn't know I was so versatile. What am I saying? Of course you did!

CALI or TESSA?

I have to choose? They're both my girls. (But Cali, definitely Cali. Just keep it under your hat, yeah? I like to play hard to get! PS It's Cali!)

WHISKERS or THE DREAD-YACHT?

Look, Whiskers is OK for a giant chicken, but nothing beats my big beautiful boat. The *Dread-Yacht* every time . . . unless you have something faster I could pilot?

COMPUTER NAVIGATION or MAPS?

Neither! Don't need 'em! I have an uncanny sense of direction, even when completely and utterly lost.

HUGO or MAGS?

Hugo's my main man! Well, after me, that is! It's just a shame the little fella gets so airsick every time he flies with me. Strange that!

SKYSTONES or SKYSTONES SMASH?

To be honest, I'm kinda great at both. What? You heard I lost to Dreadbeard yesterday? Hey, I let the guy win. I'm big-hearted like that.

ENCHILADAS or CHILLI?

Hang on! Isn't there chilli *in* enchiladas? That was a trick question! You have to get up earlier than that to pull the goggles over Captain Flynn's eyes! You have made me hungry again, though.

BUZZ or SHARKFIN?

Hmmmm. Sharkfin does have an awesome ship, but Buzz is OK, I guess – although, does the old-timer look kinda weird to you?

MODESTY or BOASTING?

Oh, modesty every time. I can't stand people who blow their own trumpet. Actually, *I* can play the trumpet. I can play the trumpet better than anyone else in Skylands. In fact, I'm probably better than the guy who invented trumpets in the first place. So, yeah – modesty.

BOOM or ULTIMATE BOOM?

What about an Ultra-Mega-BOOM! Ha! You weren't expecting that, were you?

ESCAPE FROM GOLD

FINISH
YOU'RE FREE!

36

35

26

27

28

25

23

22

13

14

15

12

11

10

START
GET RUNNING!
THE GOLDEN
QUEEN IS
COMING!

2

3

MOUNTAIN!

Danger, Mabu Defence Force. The Golden Queen is after you! Can you escape her clutches before she transforms you into solid gold?

34	33	32
29	30	31
21	20	19
16	17	18
9	8	7
4	5	6

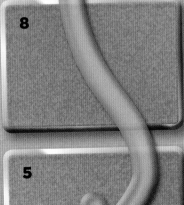

You'll need:
- Counters (why not use coins or sweets?)
- A dice

How to play:

1. Place your counters on the starting square.
2. Roll the dice. The player who rolls the highest number goes first.
3. Take turns to roll the dice. Move forward the number thrown.
4. If you land on a super bounce pad, follow the arrows up the board.
5. If you land on a goo trail, slide all the way down to the bottom.
6. If you land on a square with a Chompy Worm, MISS A GO! Aaargh!

Good luck!

What's Your Skylander Name?

Find your initials to discover your Skylander name! Then use the first letter of your school's name to see which Element you are!

FIRST NAME	SURNAME	ELEMENT
A Invisible	A Flyer	A Air
B Gear	B Tornado	B Undead
C Fright	C Boom	C Earth
D Mighty	D Storm	D Magic
E Stink	E Knight	E Light
F Wild	F Bot	F Water
G Time	G Shadow	G Life
H Flame	H Wonder	H Dark
I Sonic	I Ghost	I Fire
J Astro	J Tron	J Tech
K Danger	K Naught	K Air
L Hot	L Zone	L Undead
M Lightning	M Strike	M Earth
N Silver	N Heart	N Magic
O Shock	O Phantom	O Light
P Rock	P Charge	P Water
Q Whizz	Q Star	K Life
R Mega	R Champ	R Dark
S Vortex	S Wizard	S Fire
T Crack	T Zone	T Tech
U Boom	U Ranger	U Air
V Golden	V Target	V Undead
W Thunder	W Driver	W Earth
X Slobber	X Master	X Magic
Y Blaster	Y Jet	Y Light
Z Ultra	Z Steel	Z Water

MINION MELEE

Read the facts and put crosses in the grid to work out which Skylander battled which minion in which location.

		MINIONS			LOCATIONS		
		Evilkin	Trolls	Cyclopses	The Eternal Archive	Junk Mountain	Forest of Fear
SKYLANDERS	Jet-Vac						
	Fist Bump						
	Eruptor						
LOCATIONS	The Eternal Archive						
	Junk Mountain						
	Forest of Fear						

FACTS:
- The trolls weren't found at Junk Mountain.
- A Fire Skylander faced the Cyclopses.
- The Evilkin attacked the Eternal Archive.
- Fist Bump wasn't sent to the Forest of Fear.

.... fought the .... in ....
.... fought the .... in ....
.... fought the .... in ....

MINI MADNESS

Can you work out which Mini is missing from each of these rows?

Path Master

Can you find a path through the grid crossing every word off the list? The last letter of one word is the first letter of the next. Hugo has started for you! What a generous Mabu he is!

R	O	R	L	E	C	R	E	A	K	R	C	S	N
I	H	A	C	R	S	E	B	A	M	O	H	T	A
P	C	E	P	U	E	A	K	N	G	A	R	O	P
T	I	D	T	E	Y	M	N	A	O	O	E	H	S
C	O	R	O	N	G	A	O	U	T	P	A	M	L
K	O	T	B	O	N	Y	R	D	E	M	T	E	L
Y	B	O	R	C	A	P	I	O	L	U	P	N	I
R	B	E	D	H	K	S	D	S	H	B	A	C	G
O	D	A	R	A	R	M	O	O	R	Y	R	K	N
L	I	U	G	R	A	B	U	G	H	T	Y	R	I
L	U	Q	E	O	D	O	A	E	T	T	P	T	K
I	M	S	Y	R	R	O	N	S	O	A	N	E	E
N	B	U	E	G	N	M	D	S	A	T	H	Q	U
O	U	O	S	M	I	A	E	R	U	L	U	N	E
L	S	L	U	A	N	G	S	H	R	O	M	P	D
O	Z	Z	C	L	T	H	Y	E	I	B	R	L	L
B	I	O	C	L	I	G	E	L	C	D	E	I	O
B	R	S	B	W	A	R	B	K	H	N	I	N	G
E	A	T	O	L	T	O	D	C	O	U	H	T	S
R	T	O	O	T	H	O	S	I	M	P	C	H	E

AURIC
CHOMP CHEST
DARK SPYRO
DROBOT
ECHO
ERUPTOR
EYE BRAWL
EYE SCREAM
EYE SMALL
GILLMEN
GOLDEN QUEEN
HOOD SICKLE
KRYPT KING
LIGHTNING ROD
LOB-STAR
LUMINOUS
MAGNA CHARGE
MAGS
NATTYBUMPO
NAUTELOIDS
OCCULOUS
ONK BEAKMAN
OOGA ORCS
ORACLE
RIPTIDE
RIZZO
ROCKY ROLL
SHREDNAUGHT
SHROOMBOOM
SLOBBER TOOTH
SNAP SHOT
SQUIDBEARD
T-BONE
TESSA
THREATPACK
THUMPLING
THUNDERBOLT

The letters you *don't* use will spell out the name of a Skylanders Mini, but which one? _ _ _ _ _ _

32

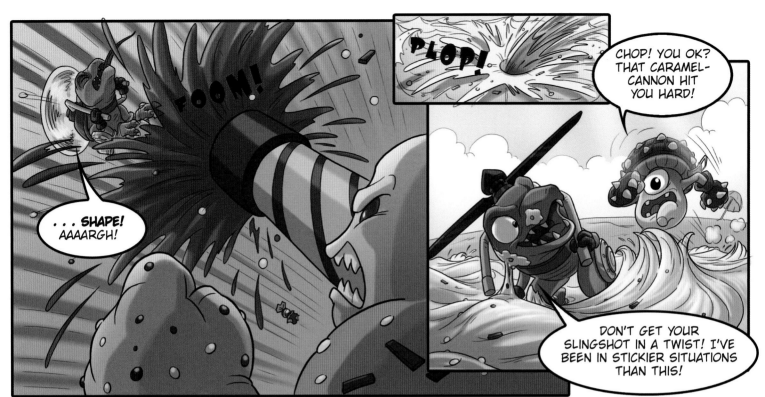

SPOT THE DIFFERENCE

Can you spot all ten differences between these two pictures?

37

WIND-UP

Origin: Created by a time-obsessed toymaker! Wind-Up spent his early life helping the temporal toyshop run like clockwork. When the toymaker accidentally sparked off a time-storm, Wind-Up sprang into action to defend his home from chrono-crazed cyclopses!

Personality: Punctual Wind-Up is always on time, no-matter what. Bursting with energy, the Tech Skylander is also a master strategist, able to spin a plan at a moment's notice.

Special abilities: His spring-loaded boxing gloves leave enemies battered.

Did you know? To relax, Wind-Up plays really loud cymbals. Really, *really* loud cymbals.

ROCKING

BOUNCER

Origin: Long ago, Bouncer was the most famous Roboto-Ball player in all of Skylands. When the evil Arkeyans banned Roboto-Ball, Bouncer was forced to work as a guard in the Mabu Mines, but rebelled against his masters to save his fans!

Personality: Fast-talking Bouncer is always full of get-up-and-go. He can't help looking on the bright side of life.

Special abilities: Look out for those fingers! They fire bouncy balls!

Did you know? Bouncer was one of the legendary Giants who defeated the Arkeyan king.

JAWBREAKER

Origin: The Sky Train was an epic engine that travelled to thousands of islands every day. When Gear Trolls attempted to hijack the celestial choo-choo for their own evil ends, one worker robot made sure they reached the end of their line. His name – Jawbreaker!

Personality: Jawbreaker loves working to a schedule. Nothing makes him happier than rules and regulations – other than pounding Gear Trolls, of course.

Special abilities: His Traptanium fists pack quite a punch!

Did you know? Most Sky-train robots can't think for themselves. Jawbreaker is one of a kind!

GEARSHIFT

Origin: Invented by King Mercurus of the kingdom of Metallana, Gearshift was brought up as a princess. However, she preferred oily workshops to royal duties. The lessons she learnt toiling away in Metallana's underground machines came in handy when she saw off a squad of Undead Stormriders.

Special abilities: Gearshift wields the ancient emblem of her robot race, the Great Gear, and uses it to slice through evildoers everywhere.

Did you know? No matter how oily she gets, Gearshift's pristine paintwork magically cleans itself. Handy.

ROBOTS

DRILL SERGEANT

Origin: Buried alive, Drill Sergeant slumbered for generations after the fall of the Arkeyan Empire, but was woken when Terrafin burrowed straight into him. By Arkeyan custom, Drill Sergeant was obligated to obey the Dirt Shark for all time – until Terrafin ordered him not to!

Special abilities: The Arkeyan bulldozer's drills can cut their way through mountains like a knife through sheep-wool butter.

Personality: Drill Sergeant possesses an incredibly logical mind, which means that even in times of great peril he never gets wound up!

Did you know? Because of his programming, Drill Sergeant calls everyone 'Sir' – even girls!

MAGNA CHARGE

Origin: No one knows why Magna Charge was created with a giant magnet for a head. The trouble was that his fellow Ultron robots couldn't help but be attracted to him – literally. Magna Charge was exiled to a distant island until he could control his magnetic powers.

Abilities: Magna Charge is a master of magnetism, able to attract or repel enemies at will.

Personality: Magna Charge just wants to belong and is fiercely loyal. When riled, this strong-willed warrior is a force to be reckoned with.

Did you know? During his exile, Magna Charge's entire robot race was destroyed. He still doesn't know who was responsible!

Skylanders Story-Tronic!

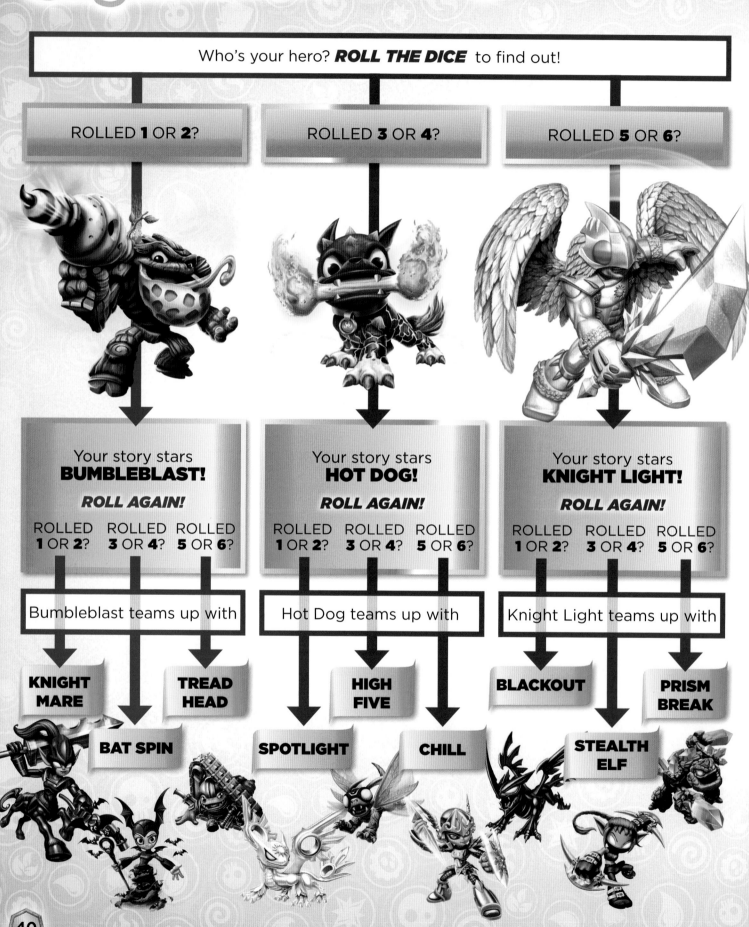

Who's your hero? **ROLL THE DICE** to find out!

ROLLED **1** OR **2**?

ROLLED **3** OR **4**?

ROLLED **5** OR **6**?

Your story stars
BUMBLEBLAST!

ROLL AGAIN!

ROLLED **1** OR **2**?   ROLLED **3** OR **4**?   ROLLED **5** OR **6**?

Your story stars
HOT DOG!

ROLL AGAIN!

ROLLED **1** OR **2**?   ROLLED **3** OR **4**?   ROLLED **5** OR **6**?

Your story stars
KNIGHT LIGHT!

ROLL AGAIN!

ROLLED **1** OR **2**?   ROLLED **3** OR **4**?   ROLLED **5** OR **6**?

Bumbleblast teams up with

Hot Dog teams up with

Knight Light teams up with

KNIGHT MARE

TREAD HEAD

HIGH FIVE

BLACKOUT

PRISM BREAK

BAT SPIN

SPOTLIGHT

CHILL

STEALTH ELF

Want to make up your own Skylanders story? Then use Hugo's story-tronic generator! All you need is a dice! Roll it now to get started!

Write your adventure here!

_____ and _____

are searching for the Legendary

_____

when they find themselves face to face with

_____!

ROLL AGAIN to find out which Legendary Treasure they're searching for!

ROLLED 6?	ROLLED 5?	ROLLED 4?	ROLLED 3?	ROLLED 2?	ROLLED 1?
They're searching for the **LEGENDARY EEL PLUNGER!**	They're searching for the **LEGENDARY HIPPO HEAD!**	They're searching for the **LEGENDARY ROCKET!**	They're searching for the **LEGENDARY SAW BLADE!**	They're searching for the **LEGENDARY BUBBLE FISH!**	They're searching for the **LEGENDARY PARACHUTING MABU!**

ROLL AGAIN to discover which Doom Raider will try to stop them!

ROLLED **1**?
DREAMCATCHER

ROLLED **2**?
CHEF PEPPER JACK

ROLLED **3**?
DR. KRANKCASE

ROLLED **4**?
WOLFGANG

ROLLED **5**?
GOLDEN QUEEN

ROLLED **6**?
KAOS

Do the skylanders win the battle? **ROLL AGAIN** to find out!

ROLLED **6**, **5** OR **4**?
BOO, THEY LOSE!

ROLLED **3**, **2** OR **1**?
YAY, THEY WIN!

41

MONSTER SURVIVAL GUIDE

Snap Shot is the greatest monster hunter of all time. Who better to introduce you to Skylands' most deadly beasts? Pay attention – your life may well depend on it!

AWWW! | AARGH!

SCARE-O-METER
Fill in each creature's scare-o-meter to show how terrifying they actually are!

Cuddles
Awww! They look so cute and just want to give you a hug. WRONG! A cuddle from this long-armed pest will crush you!

Habitat: Anywhere you least expect them.

Survival tip: Keep Cuddles at arm's length at all times.

AWWW! | AARGH!

Snozzlers
These long-nosed fliers are nothing to sneeze at, especially when they blow out booming boogers. Disgusting!

Habitat: Above your head right now! (Ha! Made you look!)

Survival tip: All that flapping means Snozzlers tire easily. Wait until they're resting and then blow that nose away!

AWWW! | AARGH!

Chompies
New species of Chompies are being discovered every day – usually when they bite someone. Goo Chompies are the latest mad mutation. They explode into gunge when hit.

Habitat: Everywhere!

Survival tip: Look for Chompy Pods. Take out the pesky plants to stop Chompies being spawned.

AWWW! | AARGH!

Cyclops Dragon
These monstrous mothers surround themselves with their eyeball brood for protection. Watch out that they don't roll their eyes at you!

Habitat: Murky marshes and spooky zones.

Survival tip: Taking out the wild-staring babes will bring a tear to the dragon's eye.

AWWW! | AARGH!

Trog Wanderers

These ghastly ghouls love nothing more than tucking into their food. Unfortunately, you're on the menu. The more they bite, the bigger they grow.

Habitat: Graveyards and terrible tombs.

Survival tip: Bop a Trog on the nose and it'll shrink away to nothing.

AWWW!   AARGH!

AWWW!   AARGH!

Chompy Worms

The largest Chompies ever discovered. Have you seen the size of those teeth? They love to lurk beneath the sand so that they can snack on unsuspecting sunbathers.

Habitat: Anywhere there is sand.

Survival tip: Blast off a Chompy Worm's shell and it'll transform into a not-so-beautiful butterfly and fly away.

Rainfish

Closely related to the mythical Leviathan, this freaky fish brings bad weather wherever it goes. Oh, and it eats everything in its path, too. It's not advisable to keep these as pets.

Habitat: Stormy seas.

Survival tip: Rainfish are particularly partial to industrial waste. Lure them into a trap with a barrel or two of the toxic treat.

AWWW!   AARGH!

MONSTER MASH

Which of these creatures doesn't fit into Snap Shot's grid?

Chompies
Rainfish
Snozzlers
Trogs
Cuddles

Potion Maker!

Pop Fizz is best known for his crazy concoctions (and for turning into a hairy beast, of course!) Why not mix your own potions?*

You'll need:

- Three jam jars
- A tray
- Baking soda
- Food colouring
- Washing-up liquid
- Vinegar

Don't try drinking your baking soda potions. They'll taste almost as rank as Bottom-feeding Suction-eel-flavoured Soda!

1 Place three jam jars on to the tray.

2 Fill them with baking soda.

3 Add a drop or two of food colouring to each jam jar. Try using a different colour for each potion.

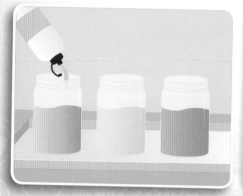

4 Add a quick squirt of washing-up liquid.

5 Pour vinegar into each jar. Prepare to watch your potions bubble and boil over! You'll be glad you used that tray!

6 If there are clumps of baking soda still in the jars, plop them into the potion mixture that's on the tray, and watch them splash and fizz!

* Ask a parent/guardian's permission, and make sure they supervise you while making your Pop Fizz potions! Maybe they could make one too?

SMASHED!

Someone has accidentally smashed Pop Fizz's favourite potion bottle! Solve the clues to find out who it was.

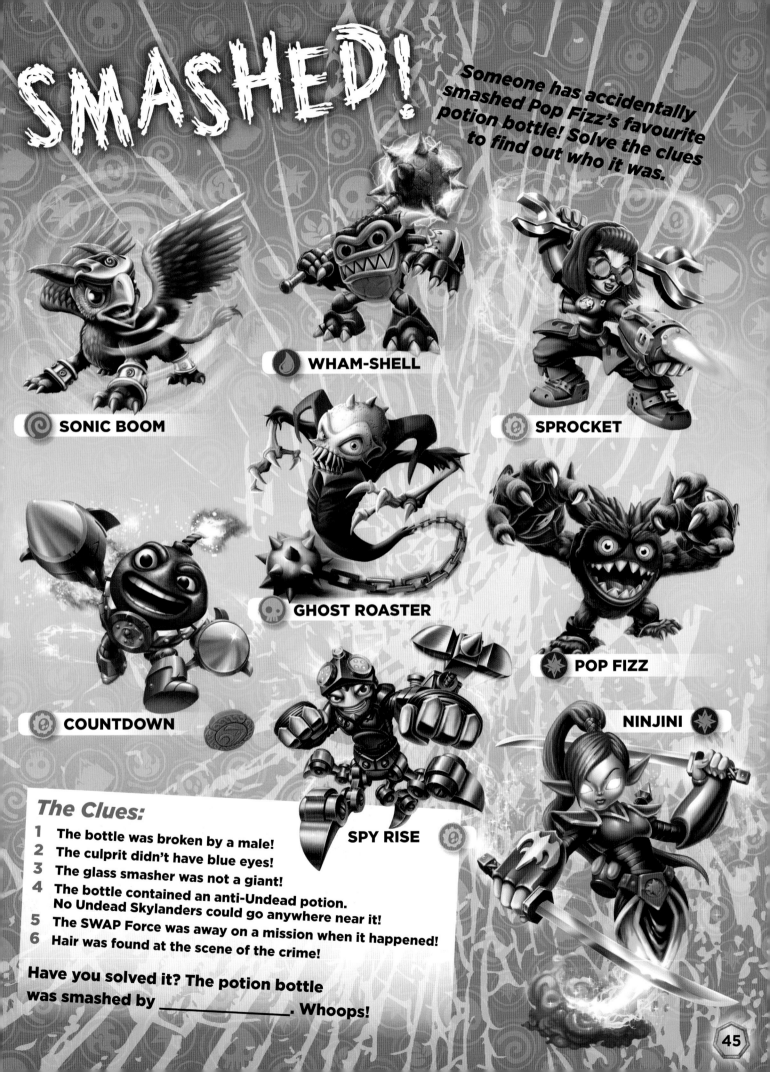

WHAM-SHELL

SPROCKET

SONIC BOOM

GHOST ROASTER

POP FIZZ

COUNTDOWN

SPY RISE

NINJINI

The Clues:

1. The bottle was broken by a male!
2. The culprit didn't have blue eyes!
3. The glass smasher was not a giant!
4. The bottle contained an anti-Undead potion. No Undead Skylanders could go anywhere near it!
5. The SWAP Force was away on a mission when it happened!
6. Hair was found at the scene of the crime!

Have you solved it? The potion bottle was smashed by _____. Whoops!

Enemy Assembly

These minions, enemies and all-round crooks are causing havoc all over Skylands. Fit them into the grid so the Skylanders can keep an eye on them!

SHEEP CREEP

PIPSQUEAK

KRANKENSTEIN

GOLDEN QUEEN

WOLFGANG

MESMERALDA

BLASTERTRON

TUSSLE SPROUT

BOMB SHELL

GULPER

DREAMCATCHER

GRAVE CLOBBER

BUZZER BEAK

CHEF PEPPER JACK

GRINNADE

BROCCOLI GUY

THREATPACK

CHILL BILL

Across

5 Rocks by, never rolls over (8)
7 You'll be crying for your mummy when this mummy strikes (5, 7)
11 A drilling machine that loves to sing (5, 1)
13 A walking time bomb (8)
15 Don't get sucked into his vacuum arm! (12)
16 She's your worst nightmare! (12)
20 The most evil Portal Master ever, no contest (4)
21 Two trolls in one big lumberjack machine (11)
25 His real name is Professor Nilbog (10)
26 A robot from the future (11)
27 He'll try to control your thoughts (10)

Down

1 Green and mean, but tastes delicious (8, 3)
2 An icy troll turned DJ (5, 4)
3 A one-eyed arena master with sinus problems (9)
4 His blasts will give you shell shock! (4, 5)
6 A gleaming monarch (6, 5)
8 This crab first discovered petrified Darkness (5, 3, 10)
9 Spits evil little eyeballs (3, 5)
10 If you're not a Chompy, he won't like you (6, 4)
12 A crooked copter bird (6, 4)
14 Half dog, half plant, half monster. Is that too many halves? (7, 4)
17 The smelliest vegetable around (6, 6)
18 Skylands' greatest (evil) cook (4, 6, 4)
19 He loves his soda! (6)
22 Ewe don't want to mess with this woolly character (5, 5)
23 A show-stopping spider puppeteer (10)

Do you know what Trap Masters use to capture villains? Reading from the bottom of the grid, use the letters in the yellow squares to find out!

46

CHOMPY MAGE

SLOBBER TRAP

BARON VON
SHELLSHOCK

DRILL-X

EYE SCREAM

MASKERMIND

KAOS

SHREDNAUGHT

MAD HATTERS

by Onk Beakman

PART TWO: CHOMPY CHARGE!

Torch rushed over and shook Food Fight's shoulders. "Hey, snap out of it. The Chompy Mage is controlling your mind!" he said.

The Life Skylander's eyes were spinning as he sluggishly replied, "No, the Chompy Mage is my master."

"It's these hats," Torch said, trying to prise the Chompy Cap from Food Fight's head. "That's how he's doing it. If you take it off, you'll be free to think for yourself."

But the hat wouldn't budge – not one bit. Torch rushed over to Funny Bone and Fling Kong, but their hats were stuck fast too. She was so busy trying to remove the horrid headwear that she didn't hear someone creep up behind her.

"What's this, Chompy Puppet?" shrieked a voice. "That doesn't look like one of our Chompy Caps!"

Torch froze where she stood, realizing that the Chompy Mage was peering at her borrowed Viking helmet. She forced her expression to fall, mimicking the blank look on her friends' faces.

The Chompy Mage strolled round to take a closer look.

"Why hasn't it changed?" the Mage's glove puppet said.

The Chompy Mage scratched his bearded chin. "I'm not sure," he said, his eyes narrowing as he leant in close. "And yet, the Skyloser seems to be in a trance."

Torch tried not to flinch as the Mage shoved his crazy puppet into her face.

"Who's your boss?" the puppet screamed at her.

"The Chompy Maaaage," she drawled, trying to sound like the other zombified Skylanders.

"She sounds like she's under our control," the Chompy Mage said, glaring at Torch. She didn't even dare to breathe. Surely even the Chompy Mage wouldn't be stupid enough to fall for her trick?

"Yup," the Chompy Mage announced, stalking away. "She's mind-controlled all right." He threw his arms wide. "They are all mind-controlled! By meeeeeeee!"

Phew, Torch thought. That had been close – too close. That puppet had smelled disgusting. But what next? If she was to have any hope of defeating the Chompy Mage, she needed to know what he planned to do.

A smile played on Torch's lips as an idea crossed her mind.

"Master," she groaned. "What is your bidding?"

"Eh?" The Chompy Mage said, twirling round in shock. "Who dares address their lord and master?"

Torch cautiously raised her hand. "I just wondered what you wanted us to do, now that you, you know, control us completely and utterly." She paused, before adding a hasty, "Master . . ."

"Ah, yes," the Mage said, puffing out his chest. "A good point! Listen to your master, Sky-minions, and DESTROY YOUR ACADEMY FOREVER!"

At once, the Mage's Chompy staff started glowing wildly, tendrils of emerald energy snaking out to strike the Skylanders' Chompy Caps. With the sound of a thunderclap, each and every Skylander transformed into a giant, snarling Chompy.

Before Torch could react, the bloated beasts charged forwards, teeth snapping, ready to demolish the academy brick-by-brick.

"That's it, my Sky-Chompies," the Chompy Mage whooped, hopping from one foot to the other in glee. "Chomp it to pieces! Chew the rotten place up and spit it out! Skylanders Academy is DOOOOMED!"

"I thought that was Kaos's catchphrase?" Torch yelled out, breaking her silence. "He won't be happy with you! But, then again, neither am I!"

The Chompy Mage jumped and his eyes grew wide as he faced Torch. "You!" he spluttered. "With the helmet! I knew that wasn't one of my hats!"

"No you didn't," argued the glove puppet.

"I wouldn't worry about the hat," Torch grinned. "It's the hair beneath it that's going to turn up the heat."

With a toss of her head, Torch sent the helmet flying, and her flaming hair whipped forward in a fiery flail. The Chompy Mage wailed as it curled round his staff and, with another flick, pulled the staff out of his grasp. The staff landed on the ground, and shattered as it crunched beneath the feet of one of the giant Sky-Chompies.

"Nooooo!" the Mage sobbed, as the giant Chompies immediately transformed back into angry Skylanders.

"Run!" the glove puppet yelled, but it was too late. The Chompy Mage turned to flee, only to be blocked by flying tomatoes to the left, a flurry of Fling Kong's Power Discs to the right, and giant Bone Paws erupting from the ground behind.

"Trapped!" he whimpered, as he found himself staring down the barrels of Torch's Firespout Flamethrower. "P-please don't shoot," he begged, taking a hasty step back. "I'm really, really sor— Aaargh!"

The Chompy Mage tumbled into the open hatbox that Fling Kong had slipped behind him. Quick as a flash, one of Funny Bone's giant Bone Paws brought the lid crashing down, trapping the Chompy Mage inside.

The Skylanders gathered round the hatbox, listening to the muffled sound of the Chompy Mage arguing with his glove puppet.

"This is all your fault!"

"No it's not. You're the one who fell into a box!"

"Did not!"

"Did too!"

"Did not!"

"Did too!"

"How long are they going to keep that up?" Fling Kong asked.

"I don't know," admitted Food Fight. "I just can't believe I called that rotter Master!"

"Ugh!" Funny Bone shuddered. "Don't remind me! I haven't the stomach for it. The thought of anyone finding out chills me to the bone!"

"Don't worry," said Torch with a wink. "I'll keep it under my hat!"

THE END

Fantastic Flying Machines

Tessa takes to the skies with Skylands' finest flying machines!

WHISKERS

OK, so Whiskers isn't a machine, but nothing beats my feathered friend when he's in the air! I first met him when I spotted a clutch of Chompies attacking a nest. I saw them off just as Whiskers hatched! We've been best buddies ever since.

THE DREAD-YACHT

Captain Flynn's famous, faithful airship. Originally called the SS *Look Out!*, the *Dread-Yacht* belonged to an inventor who installed a Luck-o-Tron machine. Unfortunately, the gadget went gaga and sucked all the luck out of the ship, leaving the *Look Out!* a cursed crate!

That didn't stop Flynn fearlessly taking her wheel. Well, he is so dashing and courageous and, well, just brilliant. Sigh! Sorry, where was I? Oh, yeah, the *Dread-Yacht*. It's pretty neat!

FLYNN'S LANDER

These days, Flynn also flies into danger in his high-tech lander. It even has Elemental cannons that charge themselves from whatever Skylander has hitched a ride! Sweet!

PLUS: How many hot-air balloons are on these two pages?

52

ARKEYAN AUTOGYROS

Back in the days of the Arkeyan Empire, these copters were cutting edge. Powered by pure magic, they rained terror from the skies. Curiously, Octavius Cloptimus, the Skylands Oracle, has an Autogyro. You'd think all those tentacles would get in the way of the flight controls!

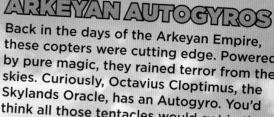

TROLL FLIERS

It's not enough that trolls cause trouble on the ground – thanks to these crazy copter-packs, the giggling goons are swarming across the skies too! Luckily, those rotor blades make the trolls dizzy, so it's a cinch to send them spinning during skirmishes.

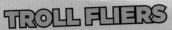

MACHINE GHOST'S WAR MACHINE

When Ermit the Hermit discovered this Arkeyan war machine, he thought he'd be able to take the battle to the clouds that he believed were planning to attack Skylands. Unfortunately, the giant flying robot turned out to be haunted . . . which scared Ermit silly! I don't know why he freaked out. Machine Ghost is the most gentle spirit I've ever met!

DROW ZEPPELINS

The Drow pack their zeppelins so full of cannons that it's a surprise they stay in the air at all! Armed to the teeth, the Drow prowl the sky-lanes looking for trouble!

SHARPFIN'S FLIER

Woah! And I thought the *Dread-Yacht* was impressive! Baron Sharpfin's airship is the fastest flier in all of Skylands. (Don't tell Flynn – he only gets upset!) In fact, I've heard the baron say that it flies three times the speed of awesome! Ka-blam!

Make a Fortune-teller!

Want to know the future? Then make Déjà Vu's Fortune-teller to find out what will happen to you or your friends today*!

How to make it:

1 Ask an adult to help you cut out the square below.

2 With the Fortune-teller face down, fold all four Skylanders corners into the centre, like this!

3 Turn it over so the Skylanders are facing down, then fold over the Element corners. Now it should look like this!

4 Fold it in half, so you can see the Skylanders.

5 Tuck your fingers beneath the four Skylanders flaps.

How to play:

1 Have a friend choose a Skylander. Move the Fortune-teller in and out the number of times shown on the Skylander.

2 Get them to choose an Element from the symbols you've revealed. Spell out the Element's name, moving the Fortune-teller in and out as you say each letter.

3 When you've finished spelling out the Element, get your friend to choose one of the four visible Elements. Their future can be found beneath that flap!

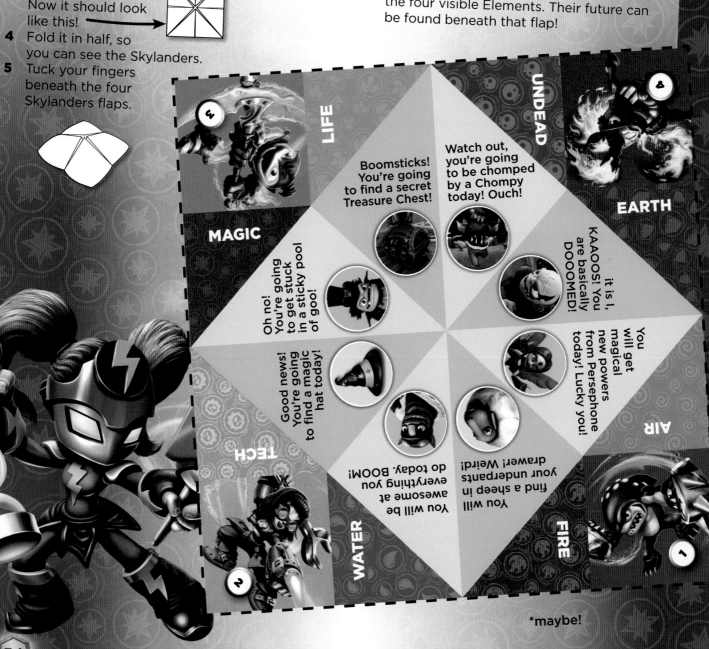

*maybe!

THE GATE ESCAPE!

Bah! Brawl & Chain thinks he's safe hiding behind these four Elemental gates! Work your way through the mazes to show him that Skylanders never give up!

START

FINISH

55

Pie Puzzlers!

Chef Pepper Jack has baked Kaos a pie, but what filling is in it? Solve all the puzzles to find out!

Entombed!

Fit the names of these Undead Skylanders into the grid to reveal the name of a Doom Raider.

FUNNY BONE

RATTLE SHAKE

GHOST ROASTER

NIGHT SHIFT

SHORT CUT

EYE-SMALL

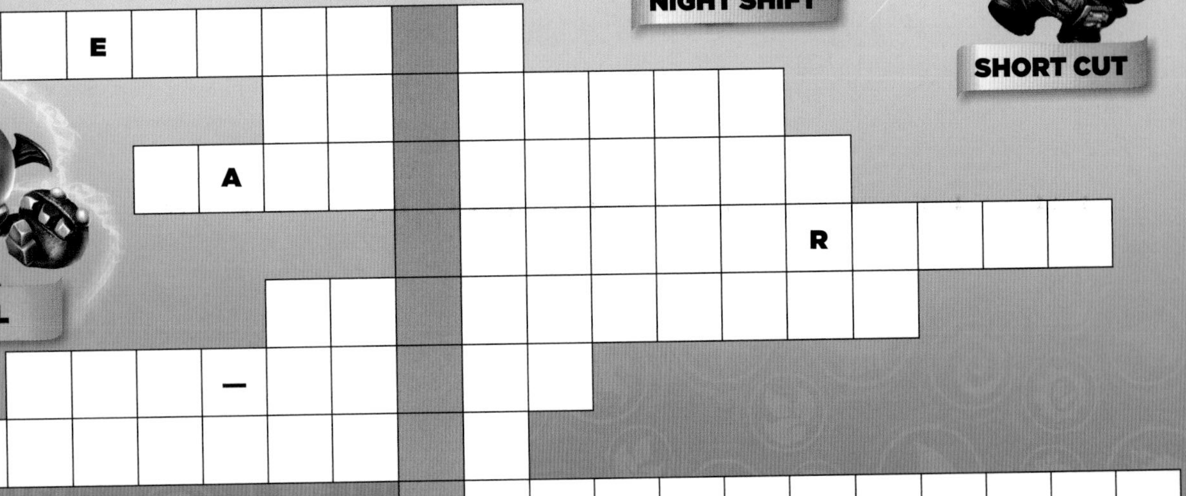

The answer is

Put the 1st letter of the answer in circle 6, on page 57.

FRIGHT RIDER

ROLLER BRAWL

Odd One Out

Which one of these Skylanders is the odd one out?

The answer is:

Put the 6th letter in circle 2, and the 4th letter in circle 5 below.

Vortex!

Which Skylander has been trapped in the vortex?

The answer is:

Put the 3rd letter in circle 8, and the 6th letter in circle 3 below.

Hidden Words

Can you find the hidden words in these sentences? They're all friends of the Skylanders.

Here's an example:
*Gulper couldn't choose between the lem**on or t**he orange soda*

The hidden word is:

N	O	R	T

1. *Even Grave Clobber likes a hug once in a while!*

The hidden word is:

Put the 4th letter in circle 7 below.

2. *Wildfire sold Auric a lion's hat*

The hidden word is:

Put the 3rd letter in circle 9 below.

3. *Sharpfin's ship accelerates safely away*

The hidden word is:

Put the 2nd letter in circle 4, and the 4th letter in circle 1.

What does Chef Pepper Jack bake in Kaos's pie?

◯ ◯ ◯ ◯ ◯ ◯ ◯ ◯ ◯
1 2 3 4 5 6 7 8 9

COBRA CADABRA'S

Let Skylands' master magician teach you some tricks!

Disappearing Salt Shaker!

What you'll need:
- A coin
- A napkin
- A salt shaker

1 Sitting at a table, tell your friends that you can make a coin disappear!

2 Place the coin on the table in front of you.

3 Cover the salt shaker with the napkin and put your hands over it.

4 Put the covered salt shaker on the coin and say the magic words "COBRA CADABRA!"

5 Remove the salt shaker and pretend to be disappointed that the coin is still there.

6 Try the trick again. It still won't work.

7 While everyone is concentrating on the coin, carefully drop the salt shaker from the napkin into your lap. Keep hold of the napkin as if the salt shaker was still inside it.

8 Try the trick again, but this time slam the napkin down flat on the table. It will look like you made the salt shaker disappear instead!

Colour Me Surprised!

What you'll need:
- Coloured wax crayons

1 Stand with your back to the person you wish to trick.

2 Ask them to take a coloured crayon and place it in your hand.

3 When it's in your hand, turn to face them, keeping the crayon behind your back.

4 Tell them that you're going to do some magic. As you speak, scrape the edge of the crayon with your right thumbnail. Some of the wax will stick beneath your nail.

5 Transfer the crayon to your left hand and then, keeping the crayon behind your back, place your right hand on their forehead. You will be able to see the colour of the crayon on your thumbnail.

6 Tell them you're reading their mind and then "guess" the correct colour of the crayon still held behind your back.

MAGIC TRICKS

Mind Master!

What you'll need:

- An assistant who is in on the trick!

1 Before you perform the trick, agree with your assistant that they'll ask you a question about a black object before asking you about the real object. Confused? Don't worry – it'll all make sense in a minute.

2 OK, gather your audience and tell them that you can read their minds! You'll prove it!

3 Ask them to choose an object while you wait outside the room. Your assistant will call you back once they've chosen.

4 Tell them to concentrate on the object, then announce that you know what it is!

5 Have your assistant ask a series of questions about objects in the room, shaking your head after every one.
"Is it the red vase?" *No!*
"Is it the green mug?" *No!*
"Is it the blue picture?" *No!*

6 Wait for your assistant to ask something like "Is it the black chair?" That's the signal you agreed earlier. As soon as you hear "black" you know the next object they mention will be the one the audience chose.

7 When your assistant asks about the next object say yes, that's the one the audience was thinking about! They'll think you're psychic!

Eleven Fingers!

What you'll need:

- Ten fingers!

1 Tell a friend that you have eleven fingers. When they don't believe you, say that you can prove it!

2 Using your right forefinger, count the fingers on your left hand: "One, two, three, four, five!"

3 Then, using the left forefinger, count the fingers on your right hand: "Six, seven, eight, nine, ten!"

4 Look puzzled and say, "Hang on, I was sure I had eleven fingers. Let me try again!"

5 When you do it again, count backwards, pointing to the fingers on your left hand and saying: "Ten, nine, eight, seven, six . . ."

6 Then count the fingers on your right hand, saying: "One, two, three, four, five."

7 Finish by saying: "There – six plus five equals eleven. I told you I had eleven fingers!"

EON'S GREAT SKYLANDER CHALLENGE

How much do you know about my Skylanders, Portal Master? Take your toughest test yet!

LEVEL 1: BATTLE CRIES!

Whose battle cries are these?

1 *"Down for the Count!"*
   a) Night Shift
   b) Crusher
   c) Jawbreaker

2 *"Your Time is Up!"*
   a) Déjà vu
   b) Grim Creeper
   c) Wind-Up

3 *"Bringing the Heat!"*
   a) Wildfire
   b) Flameslinger
   c) Sunburn

4 *"A Storm is Coming!"*
   a) Camo
   b) Gusto
   c) Thunderbolt

5 *"It's Feeding Time!"*
   a) Lightning Rod
   b) Terrafin
   c) Zap

LEVEL 2: WEAPONS MASTER!

Can you match the weapons to the Skylanders?

6 Flip Wreck

Bazooka

7 Smolderdash

Ice Javelin

8 Zook

Flame Whip

9 Chill

Sea Saw

LEVEL 3: LOCATION, LOCATION, LOCATION

Which Skylander comes from each of these locations?

10 **Popcorn Volcano**
a) Hot Dog
b) Eruptor
c) Torch

11 **Windham**
a) Warnado
b) Jet-Vac
c) Fling Kong

12 **Salt Flat Islands**
a) Scorp
b) Slobber Tooth
c) Tread Head

13 **The Billowy Cloudplains**
a) Lightning Rod
b) Blades
c) Boom Jet

14 **Arcadian Timberland**
a) Tree Rex
b) Bushwhack
c) Stump Smash

15 **Munitions Forge**
a) Ka-Boom
b) Countdown
c) Boomer

LEVEL 4: STORY SCROLLS!

Can you answer these questions about the stories and features in this annual?

16 What type of hat did Food Fight lose in a game of Skystones?
a) Artichoke
b) Banana
c) Tomato

17 Where did the Skylanders Minis visit on their field trip?
a) The Custard Lake
b) The Custard Seas
c) The Custard Ocean

18 Who did Flynn choose in his interview – Hugo or Mags?
a) Hugo
b) Mags
c) Neither – he chose himself!

19 What do the GearGolems form in *Small Wonders*?
a) A Super-Golem
b) A Hyper-Golem
c) A Mega-Golem

20 What colour are the mysterious hatboxes in *Mad Hatters*?
a) Red
b) Green
c) Yellow

How did you do?

0–5 Well, we all need to start somewhere.

6–14 Excellent work! You have done well.

15–20 Behold! A Skylanders expert! I am proud of you, Portal Master.

Answers

Pages 16–17: *Word Portal*
HAT appears 7 times in the grid!

Page 19: *Stealth Skunk*
The correct shadow is B.

Page 20: *Cali's Code*
We've nearly found the Gulper. He's hiding in the valley of the Soda Volcanoes. Get Flynn to fly over here right away! He's the only one who can help, but please don't tell him that!

Page 24: *Food Frenzy*
Hot Dog gets the watermelon, Wash Buckler gets the pizza, Short Cut gets the pancakes, and Tree Rex gets the bomb!

Page 26: *Mindstorm*
1) Yellow. 2) Four. 3) No. 4) Four.

Page 31: *Minion Melee*
Jet-Vac fought the Trolls in the Forest of Fear; Fist Bump fought the Evilkin in the Eternal Archive; Eruptor fought the cyclopses in Junk Mountain.

Mini Madness
1) Small Fry. 2) Eye Small. 3) Terrabite.

Page 32: *Path Master*
The Mini is Drobit.

Page 37: *Spot the Difference*

Pages 42–3: *Monster Mash*
Rainfish doesn't fit into the grid.

Page 45: *Smashed!*
Pop Fizz smashed his own potion bottle while in beast form!

Pages 46–47: *Enemy Assembly*

Trap Masters use **Traptanium**.

Pages 52–53: *Fantastic Flying Machines*
There are eight hot-air balloons.

Page 5: *Trinket Trail*

Page 55: *The Gate Escape!*

Pages 56–57: *Pie Puzzlers!*
Entombed!

Odd One Out
Snap Shot is the odd one out. All the others are Life Skylanders, but he's of the Water Element.

Vortex!
Chopper.

Hidden Words
1. Even Grave Clobber likes a **Hug o**nce in a while!
2. Wildfire sold Auri**C a li**on's hat
3. Sharpfin's ship accelera**Tes sa**fely away

Chef Pepper Jack bakes **sheep wool** in Kaos's pie.

Pages 60–61: *Eon's Great Skylander Challenge*
1) c 2) b 3) a 4) c 5) b 6) Sea Saw 7) Flame Whip 8) Bazooka 9) Ice Javelin 10) a 11) b 12) a 13) c 14) b 15) a 16) b 17) c 18) a 19) C 20) b